MW00650789

THE RIG RAN ON

ISBN# 1-930710-24-0
Copyright ©2000 Veritas Press

Veritas Press
1250 Belle Meade Drive
Lancaster, PA 17601

First edition

THE RIG RAN ON

STORY BY JOANNA VEITH AND EMILY FISCHER

ILLUSTRATIONS BY JUDITH A. HUNT

The sun was up.
Ed and Gus got up from bed
and ran to Ma and Pa.
They were at the rig.

Pa set a pot and pan and
mop and map in the rig.
Ma set a rug and rag and
gun and bag in the rig.

Ed and Gus fed Bud the pet dog,
and Pa fit the bit on the nag.

They were all set.

With a pit-pat pit-pat
the rig ran on and on
as the red sun set.

When Ma and Pa
and Ed and Gus
got up from bed,
the sun was dim.

Ed and Gus fed Bud,
and Pa fit the bit on the nag.

But they were not all set.
The rig was in a rut in the mud!

Pa dug in the bog,
but the mud was
on top of the rim.

The nag got a tap.
But the rig did not
top the rut.

Ma and Pa and Ed and Gus were sad,
but they were not mad.

They all dug in the bog,
and the rig got up with a pop.

Tap-et. Tap-et.
The rig ran on.

When the sun was up,
they met up with a fat man.

The man had a gun
and was set to rob the rig!

Pa got his gun.
With a sob, Ma got
Ed and Gus in the rig.

This was bad.
But that was not all.
A red man was on the rim.

Was this red man bad?

The red man upset the fat bad man.

With a mad fit, the bad man
ran and ran.

And when the fat man had run,
the red man was not on the rim.

With a pit-pat, pit-pat
the rig ran on.
Ma was not sad
as God was with them.

God was with them
when the rig was in the mud.

And God was with them
when they met up
with the fat bad man.

Tap-et. Tap-et. The red sun set.
And the rig ran on.